ON THE RIVER

Text and illustrations copyright © 1991 by Sheila White Samton
All rights reserved, including the right to reproduce this book
or portions thereof in any form.
Book design by Charlotte Staub
Published by Caroline House/Boyds Mills Press, Inc.
A Highlights Company
910 Church Street, Honesdale, Pennsylvania 18431
Publisher Cataloging-in-Publication Data
Samton, Sheila White.
  On the river: an adding book/written and illustrated by Sheila White Samton.
  24 p.: col. ill.; cm.
Summary: As each page turns, the river fills with animals in this colorful counting book.
ISBN 1-878093-14-2
1. River—Fiction—Juvenile Literature. 2. Stories in rhyme—Juvenile Literature.
3. Counting—Juvenile Literature. [1. River—Fiction. 2. Stories in rhyme. 3. Counting.]
I. Title.
      [E]   1991
LC Card Number 90-85730

Distributed by St. Martin's Press
Printed in Hong Kong

ON THE RIVER

An Adding Book

SHEILA WHITE SAMTON

CAROLINE HOUSE

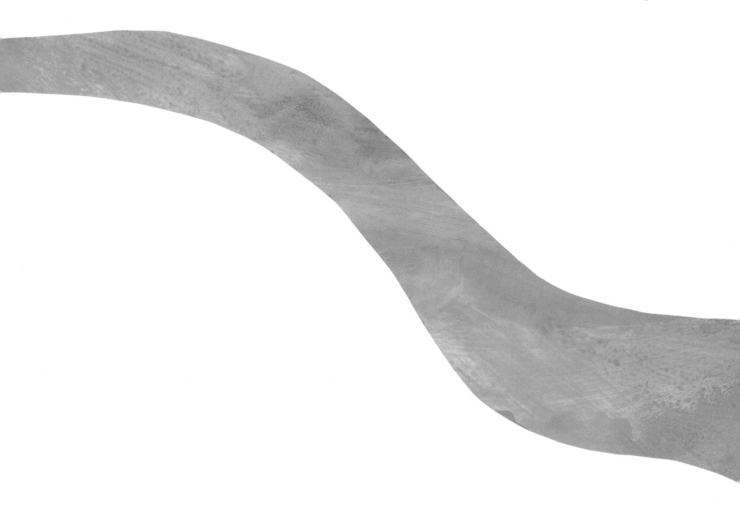

1 river

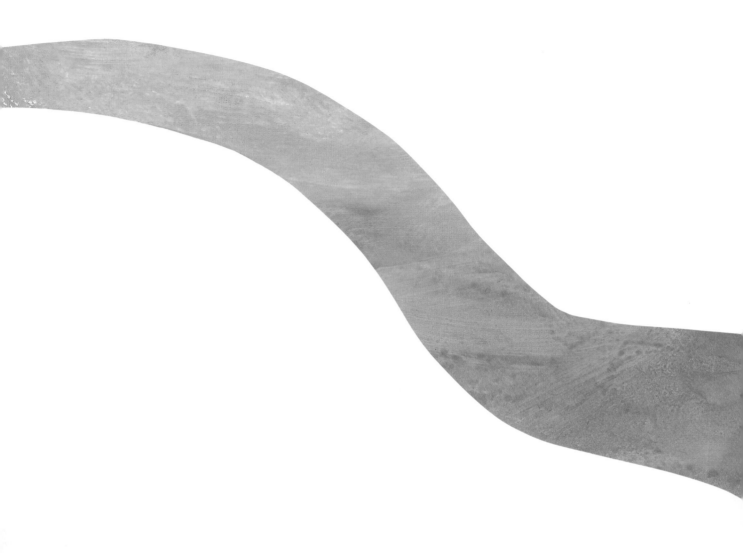

1 river
+ 1 cloud
$$\frac{}{2}$$

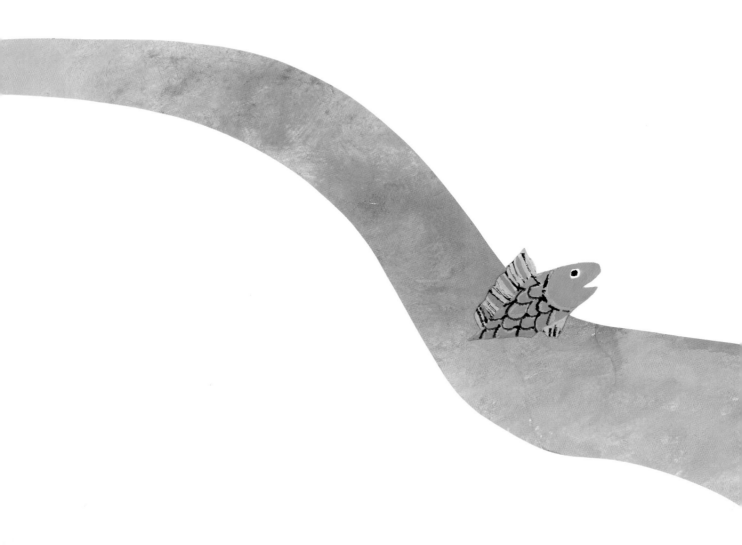

1 river
1 cloud
+ 1 fish
———
3

1 river
1 cloud
1 fish
+ 1 turtle
———————
4

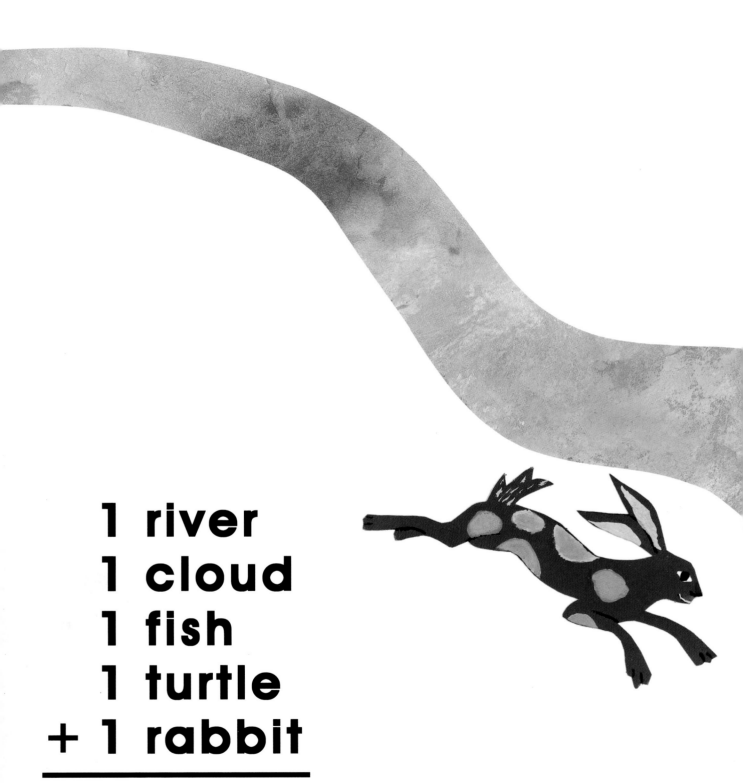

1 river
1 cloud
1 fish
1 turtle
+ 1 rabbit
_____
5

1 river
1 cloud
1 fish
1 turtle
1 rabbit
+ 1 frog
_____
6

1 river
1 cloud
1 fish
1 turtle
1 rabbit
1 frog
+ 1 duck
_____
7

1 river
1 cloud
1 fish
1 turtle
1 rabbit
1 frog
1 duck
+ 1 boat
─────
8

1 river
1 cloud
1 fish
1 turtle
1 rabbit
1 frog
1 duck
1 boat
+ 1 girl
_____
9

1 river
1 cloud
1 fish
1 turtle
1 rabbit
1 frog
1 duck
1 boat
1 girl
+ 1 island
────────
10

Picnic today!